cloverleaf books™

Where I Live

This Is My Country

Lisa Bullard

illustrated by Doreen Mulryan

M MILLBROOK PRESS · MINNEAPOLIS

For Max, who served her
country with pride —L.B.

To the teachers and staff at
Briggs Elementary School for their
constant love of learning! —D.M.

Millbrook Press
A division of Lerner Publishing Group, Inc.
241 First Avenue North
Minneapolis, MN 55401 USA

For reading levels and more information, look up this title at
www.lernerbooks.com.

Main body text set in Slappy Inline 18/28.
Typeface provided by T26.

Library of Congress Cataloging-in-Publication Data

Names: Bullard, Lisa, author. | Mulryan, Doreen, illustrator.
Title: This is my country / by Lisa Bullard ; illustrator
    Doreen Mulryan.
Description: Minneapolis : Millbrook Press, [2017] | Series:
    Cloverleaf books—Where I live | Includes bibliographical
    references and index. | Audience: Age 5–8. | Audience:
    Grades K to 3.
Identifiers: LCCN 2015048983 (print) | LCCN 2016010988
    (ebook) | ISBN 9781467795241 (lb : alk. paper) | ISBN
    9781467797351 (pb : alk. paper) | ISBN 9781467797368
    (eb pdf)
Subjects: LCSH: United States—Juvenile literature. | Pen pals—
    Juvenile literature.
Classification: LCC E156 .B85 2017 (print) | LCC E156 (ebook) |
    DDC 973—dc23

LC record available at http://lccn.loc.gov/2015048983

Manufactured in the United States of America
1-38723-20637-3/4/2016

TABLE OF CONTENTS

Chapter One

A New Pen Pal

I got an e-mail from my new pen pal! We're learning about countries in school. We each have a pen pal from a different country. My pen pal is from Morocco!

"Dear Will," my pen pal writes, "My name is Abdou. I live in Rabat. It's the capital city of Morocco. Our government is here. So is our king. Please write back about your country soon!"

A country is a section of land with its own government. Most countries cover a large area.

I'm excited to have a new friend! I start an e-mail to tell Abdou about the United States.

I add this picture of Washington, DC. It's my country's capital. My family took a trip there last summer. Mom told me all about the president and lawmakers who work there.

Every country has its own flag and its own capital. Many capitals are well-known cities, like Paris, France, and Tokyo, Japan.

"The United States doesn't have a king," I write to Abdou. "The president is our leader. Mom says the people choose the president. I guess that means the people are in charge!"

I add another photo to my e-mail. "Here's a picture of the White House. The president works there. He lives there too. Did you know the White House has a bowling alley and a movie theater?"

Different countries have different kinds of governments. In some countries, the people are included in decisions. in other countries, the people do not have much power.

Mom opens another photo. "Remember the Capitol Building? People from each of the fifty states choose leaders to send to Washington, DC. Those leaders work in this building. They make laws for the whole United States."

"Just like you make rules for our whole family!" I say.

Chapter Two

All Kinds of Countries

Mom hands me our globe. "Here's something else to tell Abdou: People have moved to the United States from all around the world. Some families came long ago. Others came recently."

Mom says that our family members came from lots of different countries, like Sweden, Samoa, Mexico, and Brazil.

We find those countries and Morocco on the globe. Countries come in lots of sizes!

There are close to two hundred countries in the world. Russia is the country with the most land. China is the country with the most people.

Our globe is bumpy and smooth to show high and flat places. I rub my fingers over it. "Morocco has lots of mountains," I say.

Then I touch some islands called the Maldives. Mom tells me they make up the flattest country in the world.

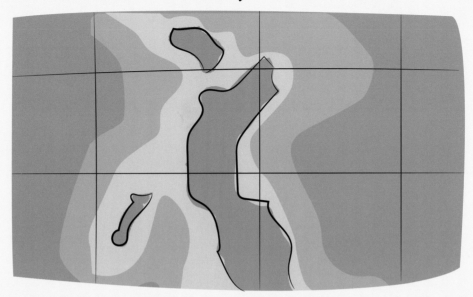

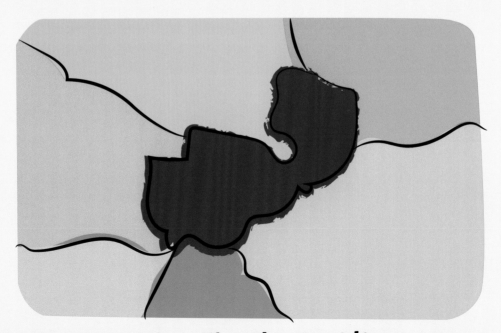

"Some countries, like the Maldives, are surrounded by water," says Mom. "Other countries, like Zambia, are surrounded by land."

We learned in school that different countries have different climates. That's the kind of weather they usually have. "Part of Morocco is desert, so I bet it's hot and dry," says Mom.

"You can tell Abdou that parts of the United States are hot and dry too," she says.

"And other parts of the United States get tons of rain, right?" I say. I want to ask Abdou how much it rains in his part of Morocco.

Ethiopia, Iran, and Jamaica are known for being hot countries. Russia, Canada, and Mongolia are known for being cold.

Chapter Three

Off to Morocco

I look for more pictures of my country to send to Abdou. I find photos of the Space Needle and the Gateway Arch.

Each country has landmarks that are special places to visit and see.

I find Mount Rushmore. I want Abdou to see the Grand Canyon and the Statue of Liberty too.

I've told Abdou a lot about my country. I say good-bye and hit Send. My e-mail is off to Morocco! Tonight I'll think of questions for Abdou. Then tomorrow, I can send another e-mail.

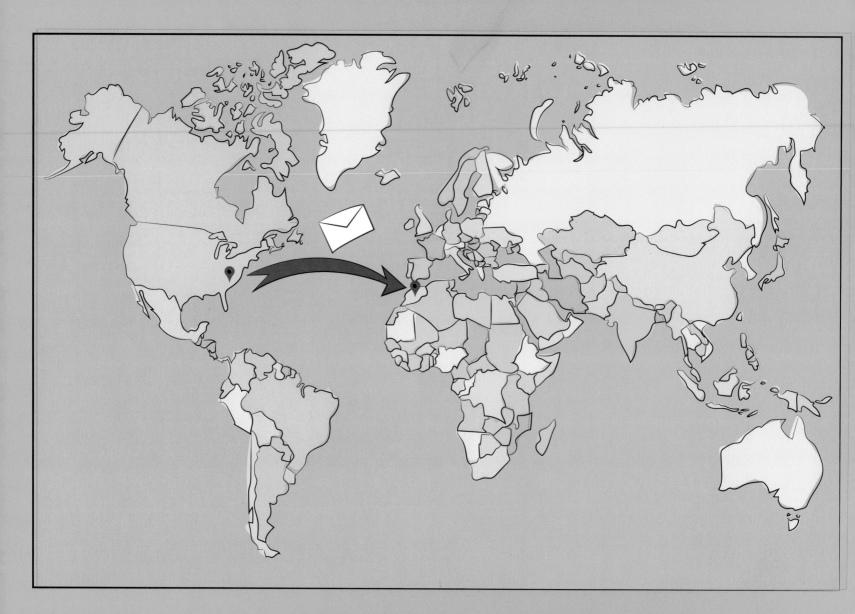

I hope I can visit Morocco someday. And maybe someday, Abdou can visit my country too!

Try it: United States Map Hunt

Will puts some photos of US landmarks in his e-mail to Abdou. Can you find these landmarks on this map of the lower forty-eight United States?

Can you find these same places in the story's pictures too?

- Gateway Arch
- White House
- Statue of Liberty
- Grand Canyon
- Seattle Space Needle
- Mount Rushmore

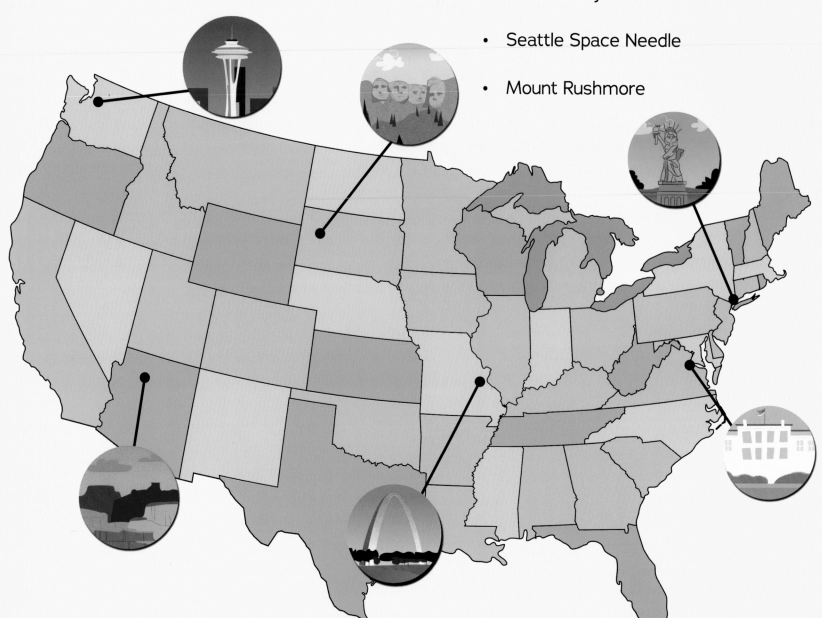